I0712751

JAMAREON'S DRUM
The
Colleton
Spiritualaires
Written by: Carolyn Williams Wilson

Jamareon's Drum

Written by: Carolyn Williams Wilson

Published by Wade Christian Publishing LLC
www.wadepublishers.com
info@wadepublishers.com

Jamareon's Drum
Written by Carolyn Williams Wilson
Illustrated by Hadia Mir

ISBN: 979-8-9857363-3-5

This book is dedicated to all the young musicians in my family:
Ta-ri Wilson (drums & keyboard), Trey Wilson (drums & trumpet),
Todd Wilson (keyboard & saxophone), Travis Wilson (keyboards),
Gean Johnson III (drums, keyboard, bass guitar & lead guitar), and
the inspiration for this book, Jamareon Johnson (drums & keyboard).
I also give a special dedication to Trevor Williams for his artistic talent.

Jamareon likes the sound of drums.

With a drumstick in each hand,
Look out, here he comes!

tap tap
boom boom
To boom boom,tap tap ,ping ping ping!

Jamareon beats on everything!

At his great grandparents' house, he taps for hours!

His drum this time is grandma's coffee table and flowers.
With a tap-to, tap-to,tap tap tap!

Grandma Evelyn yells "Jamareon! Don't break that!"

With a "tap-to,tap-to,boom boom boom!"

Grandaddy Frank sends Jamareon out of the room.

Just two years old with drumsticks in each hand,
he keeps up the beat with Papa's gospel band.

Tapping on the pews and on his mama's knee,
anything anywhere can be a drum, you see.

Now church is over,look out here he comes,
to tap-a-tap,tap-a-tap,tump-a-tump-tum!

With his tiny little legs barely reaching the floor,
his Mama loudly shouts "go Jamareon go!"

With rhythm and style, he plays so well,
as his sticks hit the cymbals and clang on the bell.

After playing for a while mom says "Jamareon let's go."
With a shake of his head,he says "no no no!"

Whether tapping on the windows or tapping on the seats, everywhere he goes, Jamareon makes a beat.

Wherever you may be, if you hear that rhythmic sound of a rat-a-tat-tat, Jamareon is somewhere around.

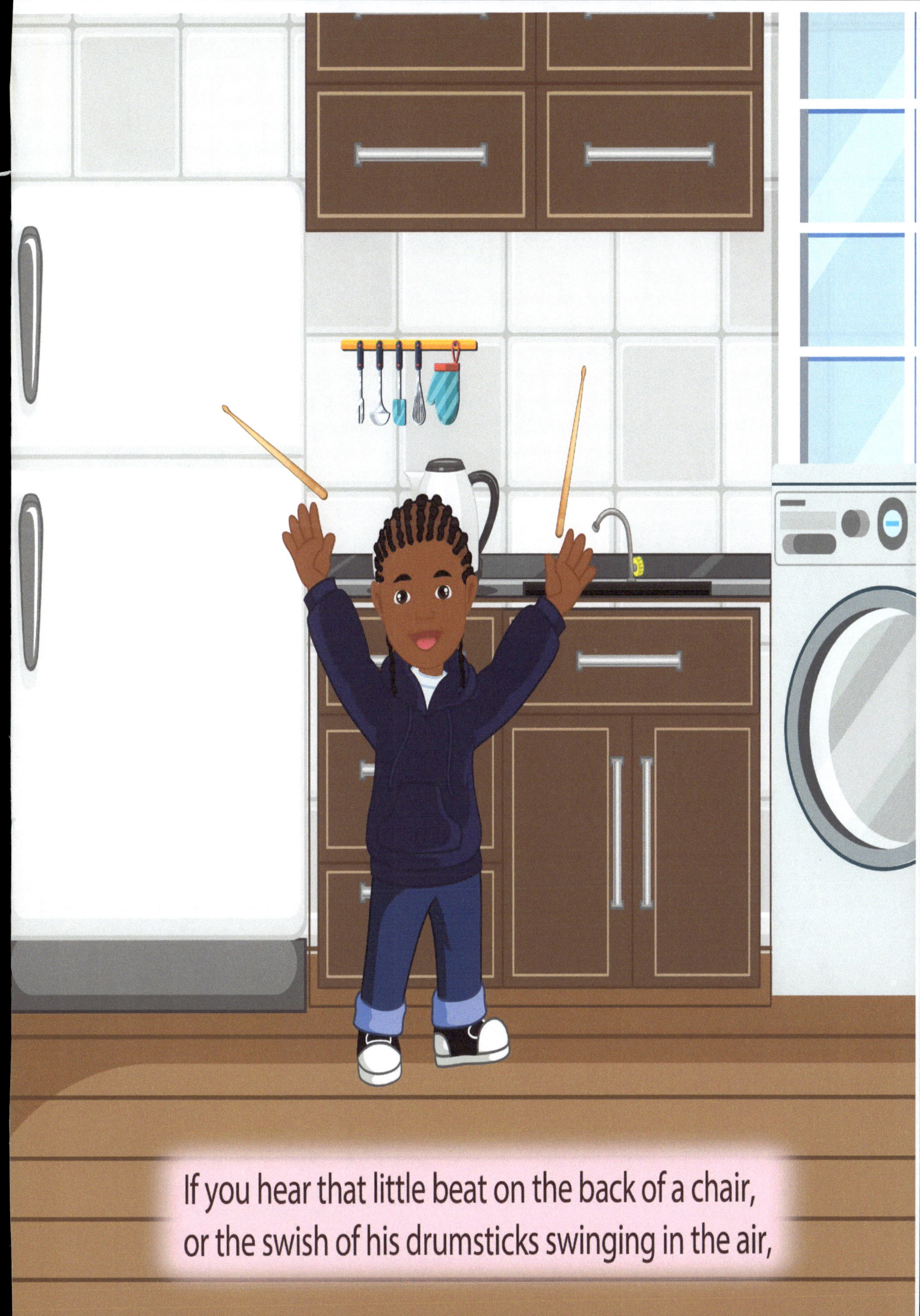

If you hear that little beat on the back of a chair,
or the swish of his drumsticks swinging in the air,

With a tap-to, tap-to, ping, tum-tum,
that's just Jamareon Johnson playing
his anything drum!

Jamareon Johnson

About the Author

Carolyn Williams Wilson's nickname is Cookie. Cookie resides in Columbia, SC. She is a graduate of C.A. Johnson High School. One of her favorite hobbies is reading. Growing up, Cookie would check out as many books as she could from the library and read them all! She passed that love of reading to her four sons who enjoy reading to their children. Cookie is the doting grand mother of 3 grand daughters (Grace, Gianna, and Talia) and is eagerly a waiting the arrival of her 4th grand child due in October 2022. She is the Children's Book Author of **Jamareon's Drum**, and forthcoming books: **Count To Ten With Me, My Ten Little Toes, Nooooh! Baby Baby** and **What Did Talia See?**